# Polly's Pet

By Lucille Hammond
Illustrated by Amye Rosenberg

## A GOLDEN BOOK • NEW YORK

Western Publishing Company, Inc., Racine, Wisconsin

Polly's Pet is fed up.

He is sick and tired of being pushed around and poked, of being shoved and dragged all over the place. He wishes that Polly and her brother would leave him alone.

When he is inside and feels like sleeping, they take him outside and pull him around. When he is having fun outside, they bring him in and put him to bed. They turn him into a baby and wheel him around in a carriage.

PET RULES

NO BITING

NO SCRATCHING

NO PINCHING

Polly's Pet is so mad at Polly and her brother that he wants to bite or scratch or pinch them. But the rules say "No biting" and "No scratching" and "No pinching." Polly's Pet does not want to get into trouble, so he does not bite or scratch or pinch.

Instead, he decides to run away.

One night, when everyone is asleep, he packs a few warm things in his travel bag. He takes along some peanut brittle in case he gets hungry. Then, without making any noise, he opens the window and crawls out.

Polly's Pet walks and walks until he gets tired. Just then a taxicab drives up, and Polly's Pet calls, "Stop! Please take me to the airport."

And off they go.

At the airport Polly's Pet buys a ticket to go up north. "Hurry!" says the man at the desk. "The plane is ready to leave." Polly's Pet runs as fast as he can. He makes it just in time.

After takeoff Polly's Pet eats a piece of peanut brittle. The flight attendant brings him a glass of milk and an apple. She sits down beside him and asks, "Who are you?"

"I am Polly's Pet," he says, "and I am running away from home because Polly and her brother are so mean to me."

"Well," says the flight attendant, "good luck!"

After he finishes his apple Polly's Pet dozes off for a while. When he wakes up he is surprised to find that the plane has landed.

He is up north.

Wherever he looks Polly's Pet sees snow. It is very cold, and he is glad that he has packed a few warm things.

    Polly's Pet takes a bus to a little hotel near a lake.
The lake is frozen, and he hopes to do some ice-fishing.
He also hopes to skate on the ice, and he wants to
build a snowman.

Meanwhile, back home, Polly and her brother are crying. They are sad and worried and upset because Polly's Pet has run away. They don't know where he is, and they don't know what to do.

Of course, Polly's Pet is safe up north. After a good night's sleep he makes plans for the next few days.

First he goes ice-fishing. He catches a big fish, which he cooks for dinner. He spends the evening reading a good book. At last he can do exactly what he wants to do!

The next day, and the day after that, Polly's Pet goes ice-skating. He skates all around the lake, and then he skates around the other way.

After that he builds a snowman.

There is no one to boss him around. He can do whatever he wants to do.

But there is also no one to watch him skate, and no one to look at his snowman. In fact, there is no one to pay any attention to him at all, not one person who cares about him. The other people at the hotel all have their own pets, and they are not interested in him.

He is all alone.

At bedtime Polly's Pet does not feel like sleeping. He feels lonely and sad. He misses home. He misses Polly and her brother, and he starts to cry. Finally he falls asleep, but he has a bad dream. He dreams that he is lost, and there is no one to find him.

The next day he is still sad and lonely. He does not want to play in the snow any more. He doesn't even feel like reading.

He picks up the phone and dials long distance. Polly answers.

"Hello," she says.

"I'm up north," says Polly's Pet.

"Oh, please come home," shouts Polly.

"That's what I want to do," says Polly's Pet.

"We'll meet you at the airport," says Polly.

In no time at all, Polly's Pet has left the hotel and is on his way to the airport. This time he does not sleep on the plane, because he is so excited about seeing Polly and her brother again.

They are at the airport to meet him. What a joyful reunion!

In the taxi Polly's Pet sits between Polly and her brother, and they both hug him because they are so happy to see him.

At home Polly's Pet is fussed over and praised. He is
petted and stroked and cuddled, and he is given
delicious things to eat.

"How we missed you!" says Polly.

But in a few days things are about the same as they used to be. Polly's Pet is dressed up in baby clothes, and he is sitting in a doll carriage. He feels squashed and uncomfortable, and he is not smiling.

However, Polly's Pet does not mind so much any more. He is only a little bit cross and a little bit fed up. Things could be a lot worse. He is not sad or lonely any more. And even if he cannot do what he wants to do all the time, it is not so bad. When it comes right down to it, home is really where he wants to be.

After all, he is Polly's Pet.